Memoirs of a Certain Mouse

MEMOIRS OF A CERTAIN MOUSE

as told to

ALEXANDER KING

illustrated by

RICHARD ERDOES

McGraw-Hill Book Company

New York   Toronto   London   Sydney

to A

IF everyone promises to keep quiet for just a little while, I will try to tell you about the most important things that have happened to me since the early part of this year.

First of all, as you can plainly see, I'm a white mouse nearly six inches long (from the tip of my nose to the tip of my tail), and until last March, I used to be employed at the National Research Laboratories, in a building on the West Side of town, right near one of the entrances to the park. I worked at that laboratory together with a Doctor Wilbur H. Howard, and between the two of us, we used to conduct a great many important scientific experiments.

For instance, on certain days, I would run through the passages of a very complicated maze and keep going until

I landed in a spot where I would find a dish of shelled walnuts. I suppose it must be pretty clear to you that once you walked into this labyrinth (which is just another word for maze), there were a good many places where you might go wrong before you managed to find those walnuts. The doctor had purposely put in some dead-

end streets and a number of misleading shortcuts, just to see how long it would take me to get to my prize. However, after I had been turned loose in that device three or four times, I somehow managed to find the best road quite easily and came out through the right door without wasting any time.

It was like a pleasant little game between us, and after a while, Doctor Howard seemed so pleased with my work that, on some Saturday afternoons, he would even bring his two children to the laboratory, just to give us all a friendly treat. Now, then, these children were a girl called Nancy and a boy by the name of Martin. Nancy was twelve and Martin was fourteen, and I must say that the three of us seemed to take to each other quite naturally from the very beginning of our acquaintance. Martin would lift me out of my glass-walled cage and allow me to run up and down his arm; and after their second visit, I even scampered inside his coat sleeve and came out into the light again, somewhere in the neighborhood of his collar.

Nancy, who had the most delicate fingers I had ever known, would always stroke my fur in the gentlest manner; and once, when I leaped onto her arm, I could feel her trembling just a little, and after she'd put me down again, she even blew me a little kiss. You see, she was really very fond of me; but, I suppose, she had just had a feeling against anybody's creeping around on her arm. In fact, it was Nancy who gave me my official name the very first time she laid eyes on me.

"Just look at him!" she cried. "Look at his pink nose and his pink tail and those long white whiskers! Why, he's a real Pinky Whiskereeno, that's what he is!"

And that's what everybody called me from that time on. It was then, too, that she discovered I had a little black spot right on the very tip of my left ear; and, believe me, that was a surprising piece of news, even to me.

10

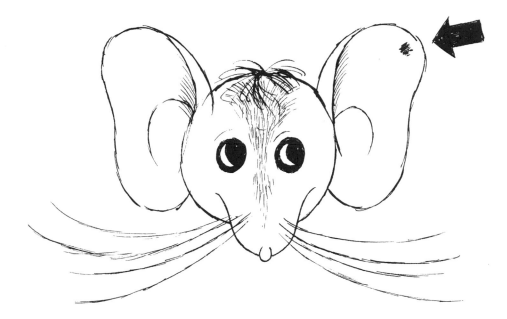

Bᴜᴛ I think I had better tell you something more about the work we were doing at this laboratory. You see, besides the fact that they kept constantly changing the paths through the maze, I also spent a good deal of time each day trying to decide between two cards, one of which the doctor had marked with an X and the other with a zero. Now, then, behind one of these cards, there would always be concealed a certain amount of food, mostly food I was especially fond of. And it was the doctor's special little trick to move these tidbits around from day to day, just to see if I would be able to remember behind which of these cards the food had last been concealed. If I jumped at the correct one, it would instantly fall down, and I was, of course, free to start munching away at my little snack. If I happened to pick the wrong one, the card would remain firmly in place, and all I earned for myself was just a small bump on the nose.

I think the doctor felt sorry for my occasional nose-bumpings, and so he eventually built us an entirely new device, which made it possible for me to just push some buttons marked X and zero, by means of which we were able to achieve exactly the same results, without my having to do any jumping at all. In short, if I pushed firmly against either of these buttons, with one of my paws, the right card would automatically tumble down, and I was at perfect liberty to indulge my appetite. If, however, I picked the wrong one, a small bell would give a clear signal of my failure. That was all. It goes without saying that I didn't particularly enjoy hearing the sound of that bell, but I think I can tell you without boasting that I really didn't make it ring any too often. In fact, in a little while, I had grown so expert at all this button-pushing that it became quite clear to me that, pretty soon, Doc Howard was bound to show up with some brand-new experiments for us to perform.

However, it was at this very point in my career that an altogether extraordinary creature made his appearance in that laboratory of ours, and in less than one week, he completely altered the entire course of my life.

I found this newcomer sitting in a cage, a wire cage, right alongside my own glass-walled container; and the very first moment I opened my eyes, on that special Monday morning, I had the peculiar feeling that something very unusual was about to happen to me.

The stranger was a large, dark-feathered bird with a

good-size beak sticking out of his head, and his eyes, like shiny black beetles, were observing me as carefully as if he were trying to guess my weight. I was quite startled and not a little frightened, too, for, after all, I had no idea how this alarming neighbor of mine might feel, either about me or about mice in general.

He must have guessed my thoughts, for he moved somewhat closer to my side and, in a surprisingly pleasant voice, said: "A very good morning to you, Mr. Mus Albus, a very good morning to you, indeed."

"Mus Albus?" I said. "Why, that isn't my name at all."

"Oh, I suppose not," he said. "I should have guessed that you would have a local name of some sort. However, I feel pretty certain that in the Latin tongue you are called Mus Albus. Mus for mouse, and Albus for white."

"You speak Latin?" I said.

"I speak sixteen different languages," said this queer bird, "and that does not include my knowledge of Muskrat, Pelican, Mouse, Camel, Wombat, and low Armadillo."

I was absolutely thunderstruck.

"May I be so bold as to ask your name?" I said.

"You may, indeed. My name is Tinto, Jacinte, Horvath, Krebiel, Maurice, Angelico, Terician, Aardmoor, Launcelot, Fahrenheit, Medmehta, Bakaar. My friends just call me Bakaar, and I do hope you will feel free to avail yourself of that privilege. As you probably already have guessed, I belong to the tribe known as myna birds, whose special gift happens to be their easy command of languages. We have been the greatest talkers in all of

14

recorded, and even unrecorded, history; and I have even heard somewhere that Alexander the Great's chief reason for crossing the Khyber Pass was to secure some myna birds for his old teacher, whose name was Aristotle. I hope it will not surprise you too much to hear that our original place of origin is India."

"I am very pleased to make your acquaintance," I said. "Are you planning to spend some time with us, Mr. Bakaar, or are you only passing through on your way to your native country?"

"I plan to remain here as long as it suits my fancy," he said. "You see, I've done quite a bit of traveling in my time, and in the course of an unusually active life, I have learned to deal pretty effectively with the rather simple locks that are generally fastened on my cages. In fact, just before you opened your eyes, I was planning a little harmless joke on you. It was my plan to join you in your glass cabin, as a special, early-morning surprise."

THESE words of his upset me greatly, since I had no way of knowing whether myna birds, along with some other feathered creatures I had heard about, were not in the habit of eating mice for breakfast.

My uneasiness must have been rather obvious, for he gave a soft chuckle and said, "You really don't have to be worried about my eating habits. You see, like most Hindus, I am a strict vegetarian. I eat no meat at all. Fruits, nuts, and vegetables are the total of my diet; although, I do confess, I have a particular weakness for all sorts of condiments and spices—most Orientals have."

I was certainly relieved to hear him say so, although I was still filled with misgivings about his playful offer to visit me. My glass container has only a flat wire screen as a top covering, and I was convinced that this astonishing bird could easily have removed such a trifling obstruction, once he had successfully managed to get out of his own cage. My little home is certainly roomy enough for all my own small purposes; but I actually trembled when I tried to imagine what would happen to me if ever this huge desperado decided to crowd himself in on me.

It was at this point of our relationship that he politely suppressed a yawn. He excused himself at once, by saying, "I'm terribly sorry, but I have been traveling for hours and hours next to a cageful of rhesus monkeys, and what a restless, chattering pack of scatterbrains they turned out to be. I didn't catch a wink of sleep all night. By the way, I don't think you've yet told me what your own favorite local name happens to be."

"You see," I said, "there's a little girl comes to visit here almost every weekend, who is called Nancy, and she

happens to be the daughter of the man I work with. The first time she saw me, she called me Pinky Whiskereeno, and that is what everyone here has called me ever since."

"I think that's an excellent and highly descriptive name," said Bakaar. "It is apt. It sounds well, and it tells a whole story. I don't believe anybody could ask more from a name."

"I'm glad you like it," I said. "By the way, have you always been a vegetarian, Mr. Bakaar?"

"Since earliest infancy," he said. "My parents were both vegetarians, and I've so far lost the taste for all meat that when I accidentally swallowed a worm that had taken up residence in an apricot I bit into the other day, I found the taste so very disturbing I haven't been able to touch an apricot since."

"I'm especially fond of walnuts and cheese," I said.

"Separate or together, these are both admirable foods," he said. "I myself am especially devoted to chutney. Also, very hot green peppers, prepared with ginger sauce, are a particular weakness of mine."

"I suppose I ought to keep still now," I said. "You really should get yourself some rest before the day's work begins."

"Don't you worry about me," said that masterful bird. "I don't intend to do any work at all for the first few days, and later on, we shall see."

"Do you have any idea what special jobs they have in mind for you?"

"Oh, it's always the usual thing," he said. "I repeat a lot of words, which they carefully write down in some book; and then, if I feel like it, I sing them some songs,

18

which they put onto gramophone records. It's hardly ever any different. But I think I hear your man coming down the hallway right now, so let's just pretend we're both dozing."

"The truth is, I'm always rather happy to see him," I said.

Bakaar looked at me for a long moment, shrugged his shoulders, and said, "Well, there's obviously no accounting for tastes." By the time Doctor Howard opened the door, the bird had tucked his head under his wing and, for all practical purposes, seemed to be sound asleep.

I WAS, of course, terribly excited. My conversation with Bakaar had filled my mind with all sorts of new ideas; and, strangely enough, all this excitement proved to be a great help to me in my experiments with the doctor. I seemed to be a good deal quicker than at any previous time, and our button-pushing routine went off in great style and took only about half as long as usual.

When the doctor had finished with me and after he had inscribed a few notes in a tall, green ledger, he finally turned his attention to Bakaar. I had noticed, somewhat earlier, that my dark-feathered friend had soon given up his pretense at sleeping and had, in fact, been watching our various experiments with the keenest attention.

Doctor Howard now proceeded to address our Hindu visitor in a clear, loud voice, taking particular pains to pronounce each word with the greatest possible care. Also, with his left hand, he pressed a knob under the table, which instantly set a nearby recording machine into motion.

For an endless number of heartbeats, that curious bird gave no sign of life at all; and then, suddenly, he cocked his beak at a neck-breaking angle and with just a single, non-blinking eye took a long and very deliberate look at that carefully talking man. When the speaker paused for a moment, to catch his breath, Bakaar quickly twisted his head around and proceeded to inspect poor Doctor Howard out of his other black and balefully shimmering eye.

After quite a long while, the doctor seemed to have had his fill of conversation for that particular morning; and as he shut off the recording machine, I could hear him muttering, rather irritatedly, to himself. "They told me this bird never stops talking," he said. "Well, I've met some of these marvelous talking birds before, and I must say very little ever came of it." Then he slammed the door, and the two of us were left alone again.

Bakaar gave a long, shrill whistle as he turned in my direction. "I've met his kind before, too," he said. "I don't intend to speak a single word to that man until sometime toward the end of next week. And even then, I'm just planning to recite some Arabian limericks for him."

"But why?" I asked.

"Oh, that's simple enough," said Bakaar. "It is my experience that you have to make them exert a little effort or they can't possibly appreciate what you're doing. You know I watched your little performance here this morning, and it is my opinion that you're just storing up a lot of bad trouble for yourself."

"Trouble?" I said. "How could that be?"

"Don't you see, once you've mastered the tricks he wants you to perform, he must immediately set about to think of new and more difficult ones for you to do. I believe you would have done yourself a great favor if you had deliberately fluffed a couple of those experiments of yours. It never pays to be too smart or too eager in work of this kind. It simply isn't appreciated. If you'd missed a few of those buttons, or at least floundered around and wasted a little time—in the beginning, at least—then he would have been genuinely delighted with you when it was all over. The way things passed off, he barely gave you a second glance. He takes your cleverness

21

for granted, which only means he'll lie awake tonight trying to figure out something really hard for you to do tomorrow. Just wait and see."

Well, let me tell you at once that Bakaar proved to be absolutely right. Two days after our little talk, the doctor brought along an entirely new contraption for me to work with. It was a toboggan slide that ended in a basin of water. The apparatus was also attached to a couple of knobs marked X and zero; but if I ever had the misfortune to push the wrong button, I would instantly slide down this dreadful chute and splash helplessly about in all that wetness. Once when I emerged shivering from my unexpected bath, I saw Bakaar looking at me and shaking his head in a most mournful manner.

Later, when we were alone, I said to him, "Believe me, this is the first time that anything as unpleasant as this

has happened to me. As a matter of fact, I expected you to laugh when you saw me getting dunked in that silly way."

"This is no laughing matter," said Bakaar. "You are still very young, and it is quite plain to me that no one has ever troubled to teach you a few basic truths about life. You must learn to play the game in such a way that no one can take advantage of you so easily."

"I just do the best I can," I said.

"Of course you do," said Bakaar. "At the same time, you must remember that this Doctor Howard is trying to teach you something. Well, then, if you learn your lessons too easily, then the lessons are bound to become harder and harder. That's just common sense, isn't it?"

"Do you want me to pretend that I'm stupid?" I asked.

"Not at all. He knows perfectly well you're not stupid, or you wouldn't be here, in the first place. He has already written a great many notes about your skill and your fine memory, and he expects to write a great many more. At the same time, if you'd introduce a certain number of errors into your performance, he'd let you do a lot of the old tricks over and over again. And why not? You've mastered those tricks, and you can do them at will. It is a pleasant and cozy arrangement all around, I think. But then, again, it may well be that I have come into your life a little too late to do you much good. At any rate, you had better get yourself under your blanket right now, before you come down with pneumonia or rheumatism or heaven only knows what else."

The next three days were a time of complete disaster for me. I slid into that saucepan so often that I finally

23

lay down in the water, hoping I could just quietly manage to drown in it. That isn't quite true, of course. I struggled and gasped as long as any strength was left in me, and when I was totally exhausted, I just squatted shamefully in that miserable puddle, not really caring what anybody thought about me.

Strangely enough, all through this difficult period, Bakaar didn't say a single word to me. I had nothing to say to him, either, because it pained me deeply that he had to be a constant witness to all my repeated humiliations.

But in the evening of the third day, he suddenly decided to talk to me again. "I'm sorry that the things I predicted are happening to you so soon," he said. "You've shown so much ability in the past that it may, perhaps, be impossible to keep him from burdening you with more and more complicated problems. Incidentally, while we are on the subject, tell me honestly, my young friend, have you ever thought of getting out of here altogether?"

"Getting out of here?!?" I said. "Why, what could you possibly mean?!?"

"I mean, escape from that glass box of yours, get out of this white-tiled room, take a good fast leap away from this ugly building, and, once and for all, try your luck somewhere out in that great world you seem to know nothing about."

H IS words frightened me more than I can tell you. "Where could I possibly go?" I said. "I was born here, right on this very floor, just two doors away from this very room. I can't fly. I can't speak any languages."

"Nonsense," said Bakaar. "The world is full of creatures who manage quite well, and I can tell you that most of them haven't even one tenth of your bright wits about them."

"I'm not very bold," I said.

"Of course not," said Bakaar. "Just remember that a great many are bold, but only a very few are clever. I've watched you at your work, and I'm ready to say that you have some truly remarkable gifts. I certainly think it is a crime to waste them in here. When I first arrived, I noticed that this building happens to be situated quite close to a large park. It seems to me that such a place would provide nearly the ideal location for shelter and possible refuge for you. It is now already nearing the end of March, and the weather has been so consistently pleasant, these last few days, that you certainly have nothing to worry about on that score. Do you, by any chance, happen to have some friends or relatives that might, perhaps, be able to help you—in the beginning, at least?"

"I have a sister at Princeton," I said, "and a brother of mine is employed up at Harvard. I heard about these two quite accidentally the other day, when Doctor Howard mentioned the work our family was doing in various places and spoke most flatteringly about all of us to Doctor Yasakuchi, the man who sometimes drops in around here for a chat."

"Well, that sort of appreciation will only get you soaking wet every day of your life, unless they eventually decide to give you some powerful electric shocks, for a change."

"Electric shocks!?" I cried. "Why, what can you possibly mean?!?"

"I just mean that, in my time, I've seen a good many unpleasant things happening in some of these laboratories I have visited. You see, I've been to three other such places before I came here, my friend, and, you may believe me, some of the things I have observed won't bear to be talked about in sensitive company."

"I'm sure you don't mean to frighten me," I said, "but—"

"Nonsense! I do indeed mean to frighten you," he said, "because I want you to fully understand your true position. I want you to gather your forces and to become master of your own destiny. Well, what do you say? Shall I open your prison door this very evening? Since the lower panels of the outside windows are left open these warm nights, you can quickly reach the street, which is only a few feet below us, and, I have no doubt, you may quite easily achieve the freedom and security of the park before midnight."

I began to tremble so hard that Bakaar finally stopped talking. I crept into the darkest corner of my box, right behind the food container, and buried my ice-cold nose in my left flank, as I always do when I'm deeply distressed. I lay there in that dismal place for quite a long time, and since my eyes were tightly shut, I didn't have the vaguest notion of what was happening around me. Therefore, I was rather startled when I suddenly heard

27

Bakaar's voice coming to me from directly overhead. As I gazed up, I saw that he was sitting on the edge of my glass cell, from which he had, quite evidently, first removed the protective sheet of wire grating. I could tell that he was looking at me with great sympathy, and I was not in the least distressed by his sudden closeness to my person.

"I am your friend," he said. "I wish you well. Don't let yourself be too upset by my words. Perhaps I have been wrong about everything, and the future may turn out much better than I have indicated."

I was greatly moved by what he said, and particularly by the way he said it. His voice was filled with an entirely new gentleness, and his whole manner was warm and kind, as never before. "I'm sorry," I said. "I know I ought to be ashamed of myself for the way I'm behaving, but I daresay you've never before had any close dealing with such a hopeless coward."

"Everyone is frightened when he faces the unknown," said Bakaar. "I myself was frightened quite often in my life—particularly in the early days. You see, I was left as a rather young orphan in a small town in India, called Chundrapore. Sometimes it was hard to find just enough to eat, and it was only after an elderly stork, a former friend of my father's, informed me that the lifelike scarecrows wildly flinging their arms and legs about in the nearby fields were not really people that I at last managed to fill my stomach in some abundantly stocked granaries which no other birds ever dared to approach. That was an important lesson for me. I learned then that sometimes it is wise to listen to some of your elders, whose past experience might prove to be of considerable value to you. Well, just as soon as I started to eat regularly, my natural high spirits came into full play, and I began to learn the languages of the creatures all about me. Not only the languages, but also their songs and their laughter, and I even began to imitate the many seemingly meaningless sounds which pervaded this little corner of earth that was my home.

"I lived, during this time, in a ginkgo tree, which stood in the center of the marketplace, and it happened that, in the shadow of this tree, two old moneylenders had set up their booths for business. I used to watch them carefully, hours on end, until I had learned the special language that accompanied their traffic, and finally I was even able to imitate the sounds of the various metals that passed through their gnarled and wrinkled hands. Because I was young and still very foolish, I occasionally amused myself by disturbing their noonday repose by imitating the subdued clatter that precious coins invariably make when they are handled by experts. When they heard these sounds, these two old men would leap wildly from their slumber, fearing that someone was trying to run off with their valuable hoard. Sometimes, when their combined fury became too much for their harassed feelings, they even came to blows.

"And so my days went by, almost pointlessly, for quite a long while, until one evening, just before sundown, I happened to overhear two swallows that had come to take their rest on the roof of a nearby inn. I heard them talking about their long voyages across wide oceans, through great forests, and over tall cities in many faraway

lands; and as I listened to them, I became heartsick
with the thought that I was probably destined to spend
the rest of my existence in that shabby and neglected
village, at the back of nowhere. That very night, I
boarded a train—that is to say, I leaped onto the roof of
one of the rumbling coaches as it passed around the edge
of the town—and after a night full of bitter wind, mixed
with smoke and fiery cinders, I landed in a place called
Mundrapore.

"I don't want to tire you with the story of my early
voyagings. Suffice it to say that Mundrapore was just

Chundrapore all over again, and this time without even
the occasionally diverting presence of my quarrelsome
moneylenders. I realized, of course, that I was quite
unable to fly great distances, as the swallows had done or
as the storks were doing whenever they felt in the mood
to venture abroad. I certainly had to find some more
convenient method of travel than the local trains were
likely to provide.

"In the meanwhile, I just kept hopping and skipping
from village to village by my own limited powers until,
late one afternoon, I happened to arrive in a good-size

town called Pakotali. As I was resting myself on a branch of a deodar tree that overhung the veranda of a large mansion, I noticed that a very colorful parrot, who was sitting on a bamboo perch right below me, seemed to be particularly anxious to attract my attention. He had

already whistled in my direction three or four times before I decided to take any notice of him. I'd already had a few experiences with parrots in the past and had found that most of them were vain and silly creatures who wanted to be flattered all the time.

"At any rate, I finally looked directly at him and, using one of the local dialects, said, 'Were you, by chance, whistling at *me?*'

"When he heard my voice, he leaped high into the air and proceeded to flap his huge red wings in a spasm of seemingly uncontrollable ecstasy. 'A bird that can speak!' he shouted. 'At last, a bird that can actually speak! Please tell me quickly, dear stranger, are you also able to speak the French language, by any chance?'

" 'No,' I said. 'I can speak several versions of Hindi and Urdu and some English, a little Singhalese and Tamil, and also quite a bit of Arabic. But, so far, no French at all.'

" 'Ah, well,' said the parrot, 'you are still a great deal better than most. I haven't spoken a word of French in nearly half a year, and I'm just perishing to say a little something in that wonderful tongue.'

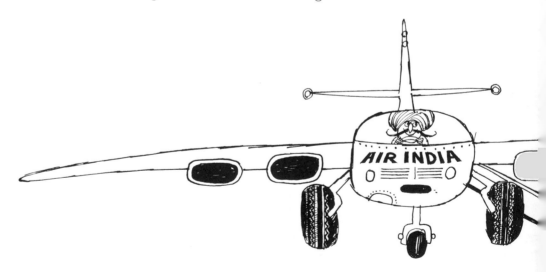

" 'Maybe someday, if I have the good fortune to travel,'
I said, 'I may be able to acquire a knowledge of that
language, too.'

" 'Ah, yes, travel,' said the parrot, rolling his eyes about
in a most alarming fashion. 'There's nothing like travel
for a bird with a lively mind.'

"And then I told him about my frustrating train experiences.

"He just laughed at me. 'Trains,' he said, 'are altogether passé; they're completely outmoded in this day and
age. You must fly by means of an aeroplane, which will
carry you anywhere in no time at all. It goes so quickly
that before you realize it, you have gone halfway across
the world.'

" 'You have powerful friends, no doubt,' I said, 'so all
this voyaging comes very easily to you.'

" 'A bird like yourself can have all the powerful friends

he wants,' said the parrot. 'You just go out to the airport, right here on the edge of this town, and sit yourself down on top of somebody's luggage; and before you know it, some worthwhile person will have adopted you.'

" 'Is it really that simple?' I asked.

" 'Of course,' he said. 'Just remember to pick out some expensive-looking luggage, and when the time comes, you speak up loudly and clearly, so that everybody will understand at once that you are indeed a most unusually gifted fellow. Believe me, they will be most anxious to have you for a pet. Of course, there are some countries in Europe where the natives shoot even singing birds— nightingales and larks and such—because they bake them in pies and eat them, afterward. But once you get to England or America, you'll be absolutely safe. Everybody there just adores birds that can talk. Follow my advice, and you will never have reason to regret it.'

"And that is exactly what I did.

"When I reached the airport, I squatted down on a beautiful leather suitcase, and when, after a little while, a young man came toward me, I said, 'Good evening to you, sir. Lovely weather we're having, aren't we?'

"Well, he nearly fell over, he was so surprised; but a moment later, he was right on top of me and clutched at me with both his hands.

"AND that is how I left India and came directly to this country. This young man was pleasant enough; but, unfortunately, he continued to take endless photographs of me. I believe that photography was a sort of illness with him, and he used to pop so many flashbulbs in my eyes that I was finally afraid I was going to become blind. So, at last, when the opportunity came along, I decided to leave him. I flew across this big city until I landed in some narrow streets, right down near the waterfront. As I was slowly winging my way through this narrow canyon, I spied a shop full of live animals, and I decided to make a halt in the doorway of this strange place. I didn't have to wait too long before someone stepped out into the street and quickly placed a large net over me.

"Later on, I discovered that the animals in this store were sold mostly to zoos and laboratories all over the country, and—to make a long story just a little shorter— I finally landed in a sunny room at a large university, where students from every imaginable place on this globe had come together to pursue their various studies. In fact, this was the very place where I managed to pick up most of my other languages.

PETS

"After a time, when I tired of this institution, I left, and by one means or another, I somehow managed to roam pretty freely across the whole of this land. Whenever the cold season came along, I always allowed somebody to capture me, and that is precisely how I happened to acquire my long list of names.

"The second time I was caught in this country, I landed with a rather sweet old lady who taught me a great number of folk songs and lullabys. She bathed me and tucked me in every night and mothered me until I was hardly able to stand it. When spring came, and I finally ran off from there, I was still wearing a colorful sweater that she had knitted especially for me. During my various

With a hey nonninoh and a ring fadiddle-oh

far-flung voyages, I landed with a movie actress, a cafeteria manager, a Latin professor, a mail carrier, a family of acrobats and, every so often, I would wind up in one of those special shops where different animals are put up for sale. In fact, it was in one of those places, in a town called Pittsburgh, that somebody from this institution purchased me for the special benefit of your Doctor Howard.

"I suppose I've come to like this part of the world well enough, although the climate is certainly pretty awful. You may well believe me when I tell you that I would have left this place very quickly indeed if I hadn't had the pleasure of running into you. Also, during the last three days, Doctor Yasakuchi has started to teach me Japanese, and I'm now planning to stay around until I've managed to master at least some parts of that difficult language, too. Who knows, I may eventually wind up in the Orient once more and, perhaps, even have a chance to give warm greetings to that noble parrot who first sent me off to the starting point of all my adventures—the airport at Pakotali. Wouldn't it be fun to return, after all this time, and offer him my very grateful thanks—in his favorite language, *French?*"

"You are a genius," I said, "and to you the whole
earth is just a simple lock, which you know how to open
with the greatest of ease. I, on the other hand, am very
lucky to get my meals every day, considering how little

I actually can do. Even so, when you spoke to me, awhile ago, about the terrible hardships that might be in store for me in this place, I suddenly had a feeling that, perhaps, I had better try my luck elsewhere. I'm awfully frightened, of course, but I also realize that this may be my very last opportunity to get out of here alive. One thing is certain: I could never dream of undertaking any such venture without your help, and so, if you are still willing, I'm ready to take my chance, right now."

"Hurray!" cried Bakaar. "Hurray for Pinky Whiskereeno, the mouse with the heart of a lion! In another hour or so, the streets will be practically deserted, and then—out you shall go, my brave camarado!"

I'm not going to describe to you all the things we said to each other during that last hour we spent together. All I can tell you is that when the time came, Bakaar assisted me out of my box and that at the final moment, he pressed his beak most affectionately against me and said, "Cheers!"

After I had stepped out through the window, I quickly scooted along the notched side of a drainpipe that led down into the street; and since our room was located on the first landing, I fortunately didn't have very far to go. At any rate, I tripped along briskly on the cold pavement, keeping close to the walls, of course, and I could feel my heart pounding so loudly that I was afraid I was going to rouse up every mischievous thing alive in that whole neighborhood.

After an endless time, when I had nearly reached the corner (the wrong corner, it later turned out), I crouched down between some badly-dented metal containers, which

47

had been stacked near the doorway of a large building. From behind this ambush, I observed, in absolute terror, how enormous engines of all sorts were racing down the middle of the street at a truly terrific rate. Well, I had been looking for adventure, and here it was right on top of me. Incidentally, these fierce creatures all had huge,

fiery eyes burning on their foreheads, and I was particularly anxious for their deadly beams not to fall anywhere in my direction.

I don't know how long I had been squatting there in the dreadful place when, to my infinite joy, I suddenly spotted two gray-colored mice coming along.

ONLY a few weeks before, I'd seen just such a mouse at our laboratory. I don't believe he was actually working on my floor, for when I had first noticed him scurrying along the ground and had called out a friendly greeting to him, he had seemed extremely upset, and a moment later he had disappeared, without even making so much as a peep in my direction.

At any rate, I was greatly cheered by the appearance of those two mice; and I took a few steps forward, so that my presence would not be too great a surprise for them. Strangely enough, the instant they caught sight of me, they stopped in their tracks, but not before the larger of the two had quickly managed to draw the younger and more delicate one quite close to her side. I noted at once that both these mice were females (a mother and daughter, as it presently developed), and the older one of them stared at me with so much obvious distaste that I involuntarily slid back into the protective shadow of the large can that towered beside me.

And then, from this somewhat safer vantage point, I decided to speak to them, no matter what the result might prove to be. "I'm sorry that I frightened you," I said, "but, believe me, I meant no harm whatever."

The older mouse at once turned to her slender companion and said, "Well, there you have it, my dear. Your papa is constantly telling you that this neighborhood is being overrun with foreign riffraff of every imaginable kind. Will you believe him now? When I was your age, this could never have happened. I could never have run into anything of this sort, even if I had been foolish

enough to roam about these streets unchaperoned for the length of a cat's age."

Deeply shocked as I was by the mother's extraordinary hostility, I took a few steps forward and said, "Madam, you really do me a great wrong. You see, I am not a foreigner at all. In fact, I was born just a few doors down, on this very side of the street, and, what is more, I have never in all my life had occasion to be out of this neighborhood, even for a moment."

"Aha!" said the mother. "And I suppose it was in *this* neighborhood that you learned to show so much of your teeth and gums whenever you open your mouth; and, I daresay, that peculiar accent of yours was acquired right here on *this* block, too."

"Yes," I said. "You see, until this very evening, I was employed in a laboratory, which is located down this

street, and all my few companions have been mice who talked exactly as I do. Quite recently, I also met a myna bird, a distinguished linguist, who sounds very much like me; but then, I suppose, *he* could easily adapt himself to speak almost any imaginable language or dialect if he just happened to put his mind to it."

"We don't want to hear anything more about your vulgar connections," said the mother, giving me an icy stare. "Our families have been living around here for countless generations, and nobody *we* know talks like *that*." Then she turned once more to her daughter and said, "I hope this will be a lesson to you, Tsi-Tsi, and that from now on you will take pains to properly mind your elders."

"But, Mamma," said Tsi-Tsi, "isn't it true that when Great-Great-Grandfather first arrived here on a banana boat from the West Indies, most of the residents of this

neighborhood also used to make fun of the way he talked?"

"Hush, you foolish child," said the mother. "Your great-great-grandpapa was one of the earliest settlers on the West Side, and you're just too foolish to realize that when he first arrived here, this whole district was still practically wilderness."

"Speaking of wilderness," I said, "I wonder if you would be kind enough to direct me toward the park that is supposed to be located somewhere nearby. I seem to have missed it so far, and I'd be ever so grateful if you'd tell me where I am likely to find it."

Without uttering a further word, the mother turned her

back on me and proceeded to walk angrily toward the nearest doorway.

Tsi-Tsi, who seemed quite embarrassed by this piece of rudeness, stepped a little closer to me and whispered, "You are heading in the wrong direction if you're trying to reach the park. You must go down to the other end of this street, and you had better be very careful when you cross over to the other side. Remember to wait for the traffic lights."

"Tsi-Tsi!" screamed the mother. "You come here instantly, d'you hear me? If you don't come along this very minute, I'm going to report everything that happened here

tonight directly to your papa. Are you listening to me, you wretched girl?"

"Good-by," whispered Tsi-Tsi, "and good luck to you." And then she turned away and ran off to join her mother.

You will not be surprised to hear that, as I looked after the diminishing form of that impulsive young creature, my heart was filled with deep gratitude for her kindness.

At any rate, I had at least managed to learn the actual location of this park; and so, without further delay, I quickly retraced my steps in what I hoped would prove to be the right road to my haven of safety. Keeping close to the grim, dark houses all along the way, I finally arrived at a much wider street; and there, clearly visible to me on the other side, were a number of trees and bushes, which (so Bakaar had been most careful to assure me) are the basic outward manifestations of every sort of park.

Unfortunately, this wide street, which I most certainly had to cross, was filled from side to side with those noisy machines I have already mentioned to you. I tried ever so hard to recall Tsi-Tsi's final instructions to me, since I was convinced that they carried an especially meaningful warning about the condition that was now confronting me.

While I was still racking my brain in a futile attempt to reproduce the exact sound and tenor of her words, the whole raging, galloping tribe of those engines came to a sudden dead halt, right in front of me.

Without a further thought, I flung myself desperately into their path, and in no more time than it takes me to tell you about it, I somehow managed to reach the other side. And not one moment too soon either, because as I was still panting to recover my breath, they were—all of

them—galloping off once more on their mad rush into the darkness.

Well, I seemed to be quite close to my refuge at last; but then I discovered, to my horror, that this park was enclosed by a stone wall—not a very high wall, really, just high enough to keep me out. Also, at this point of my life, it started to drizzle. I don't think I have ever been more miserable or felt more absolutely forlorn than during that dismal time when I crawled, sneezing and shivering, along that endless expanse of wet and forbidding stones.

At last, when I had long given up hope for any possible relief to my condition, I suddenly came to a wide breach in this terrible wall and found myself rushing into that park—expecting goodness only knows what.

I instantly discovered that the world was just as wet and cold inside as it had been on the outside; although, I must confess, I found some small comfort in the fact that the ground had become somewhat softer underfoot.

After tottering around almost blindly among a great mass of moist-fingered foliage, I managed finally to take shelter beneath a large, overhanging rock.

It took me a great while to fall asleep that night; but, in the end, my extreme weariness must, at last, have overpowered my fears, because when I again opened my eyes, it had become early morning.

The earth was still rather moist; but the drizzle had stopped, and I found myself to be terribly hungry. Some birds were twittering in the nearby bushes; and in the soft morning breeze, my fur was slowly beginning to dry out. However, as I looked about me, it became quite plain to me that there was certainly nothing edible anywhere within my reach. I tried gnawing at some exposed roots; but they tasted so terrible that I decided to get under way, at once, in the hope of finding some means for a modest breakfast.

Aᴺᴰ now comes the second great surprise of my whole series of adventures. (The first, of course, was my encounter with Tsi-Tsi and her highly irritated mother.)

At any rate, as I was tripping along through the short grass (and stopping still with terror at any unexpected movement or sound), I came at last to another stone wall; but when I looked up, I noted that it was not just a wall but a good-size structure supporting an enormous cage. Since my empty stomach had made me unusually reckless, I decided to take a closer look. So, without even considering the possible danger, I scrambled up a plank that was leaning against this structure, and a moment later, I looked inside.

Behind some iron bars and lying on a stone floor, I saw a large, fat animal that was obviously sound asleep. Now, then, whoever this creature might possibly be, it had somehow managed to scatter a great deal of food all about its cage. What is more, in a far-off corner I rejoiced to see a gray mouse nibbling away at some juicy looking carrots; and before I even had time to consider my rashness, I leaped in right beside him.

Well, you will hardly believe what followed. The moment that mouse got sight of me, he flung himself out, backward, between two of the bars, and I was able to hear, quite clearly, the loud thump he made as he hit the grassy ground below.

Ah, well, I thought, it is not unpleasant to know there are some characters loose in the world who are even frightened of me. And then, without further delay, I proceeded to eat my fill of the things that had been provided. There were really some wonderful surprises lying about that cage. In a shallow metal trough, I found large chunks of bread, which were so delicious that I nearly finished off the whole lot of it.

At last, when I seemed to have no more room left for anything else and I was only toying playfully with something that tasted very much like a young turnip, I observed, with sudden alarm, that the big, sleeping thing was sleeping no longer and was actually looking at me out of one of its large, bloodshot eyes. What is more, he seemed to be considering me very carefully indeed, and I quickly braced myself for a sudden retreat, more or less in the style and manner the gray mouse had demonstrated just a little while earlier.

So, while keeping my eyes fixed firmly on the official tenant of the house, I began, ever so gently, to wiggle my way backward toward those bars located not too far behind me.

However, in my acute state of nervousness, I simply couldn't resist saying a few explanatory words that might help account for my presence in that particular location. "I saw a great deal of unused stuff lying about all over the floor," I said, "and I only thought that, since you didn't seem to care for any of it, you wouldn't really mind if I helped myself to a few mouthfuls."

The creature just kept staring at me rather thoughtfully for a while, and then he opened his mouth and gave an enormous yawn. This greatly reassured me, because it didn't seem likely that anyone planning to do you harm was going to start things off with a great big yawn.

At any rate, while I made a momentary halt in my slow retreat, he rose onto his short, chunky legs; and after noisily clearing his throat, he again looked directly at me and said, "You seem to be new around here. I don't remember ever having seen you before. Or have I?"

"You have not," I said. "In fact, I have just arrived here this morning. I really can't tell you how greatly surprised I am to hear you speaking such fluent Mouse."

"Oh, we all do," he said. "That is the first thing everyone learns after they arrive here. Even the camel speaks it, and he absolutely refuses to learn anything else. You

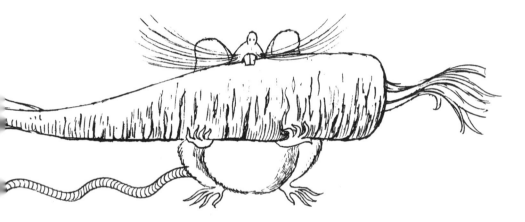

see, after all, there are so very *few* of us, and there are so *many* of you that, before long, one is compelled to acquire the official language of the local majority. Besides, if you expect people to do you any little favors around here, you simply have to learn how to tell them about your wants."

"What little favors?" I asked.

"Well, just a lot of little things, don't you know. For instance, they're forever bombarding me with great quantities of boring carrots, while just around the corner from

61

here, one can always find endless numbers of simply delicious parsnips. I don't know why they continually fling all
those parsnips at those foolish marmosets; but, in any
case, I would consider it a great favor if you would just
hop around to their cage and fetch me a few."

"I'll be delighted to do that," I said, "but are you trying to tell me that there are many cages located here
and that animals of all sorts are just waiting to be sold,
out of this shop?"

"This is not a shop," he said. "This is a zoo. We have
been brought to this place so that the public can come
and stare at us. Many people come here, every day, and
throw a great number of things into our cages—some of
them quite awful and a few of them even very dangerous.
I myself happen to be a South American tapir, which
means that I belong to one of the oldest families on this
earth. And now, if you don't mind, I'd greatly appreciate
it if you'd be good enough to see about some of those
parsnips. My throat seems to be very bad this morning,
and I find them particularly soothing to my larynx."

Of course, I instantly scrambled around the corner and
easily located the cage in which four tiny monkeys were
huddled very close together, and without saying anything
to them at all, I successfully managed to secure quite a
good-size parsnip. I had to make that same trip several
times that morning, since the tapir—whose name, by the
way, was Pancho—had a truly enormous appetite, and I
saw that he consumed his favorite delicacies without even
bothering to chew them.

Now, then, it is not my intention to tell you step by step how, in due time, I became rather intimately acquainted with most of the animals in that zoo, because I have a great number of far more important things to tell you about.

However, there is one very significant point I *would* like you to consider—namely, that the local gray mice, who roamed all over this place, were, one and all, absolutely furious with me. In fact, I heard that they frequently held meetings about me and even passed resolutions aimed specifically toward my downfall, and the only thing that seemed to work in my favor was their natural quarrelsomeness, which always prevented them from taking any effective action against me.

Even so, late one afternoon, a group of the very toughest characters among them succeeded in ambushing me just as I was passing below the tiger house. Six large, sinister-looking mice suddenly crowded me up against the wall, and the ugliest one of the lot quite deliberately bumped into me.

"Why don't you watch where you're going?" he snarled.

"I'm terribly sorry," I said. "The ground is so slippery that I must have lost my footing for a moment."

"Oh, yeah!" said this very tough mouse. "And I suppose delivering messages and carrying parcels and stuff all over the place is just a little slip of your foot, too!"

"I'm not doing anything wrong," I said. "I just do some favors for a few of my friends, that's all."

"Your friends, eh? Well, let me tell *you* something, you bleached-out hunk of mole fluff, you ain't *got* no friends around here—*see? Me* and *my* friends, *we* do all

the errand work around here, and no outsider is going to cut in on our territory. And, what's more, we're gonna make sure you ain't gonna do any more running around in this park from now on. We're just gonna give you a lesson you ain't never gonna forget."

I realized, with a wildly thumping heart, that these six dreadful characters meant to do me serious bodily harm and that they were even prepared to cause me injuries, from which I might never be able to recover.

And then, in that split second of absolutely blind terror, I made a sudden desperate lunge straight up that stone wall supporting the tiger cage, and before I'd even had a chance to consider what had happened, I landed, *plop,* right inside the bars.

It stands to reason that my enemies were completely stunned by my performance, since no mouse in the whole history of that park had ever dared go near the place where the lions, the leopards and the tigers were confined.

I knew all about that too, of course; but I had unthinkingly risked the *possible* and even very *probable* danger provided by these *big cats* against the absolutely *certain* disaster offered to me by the *big mice*.

Fortunately, I had stumbled into the cage of a tiger named Sultan, who, that very afternoon, had had one of his teeth extracted. As I scooted past him on the outer rim of his cage, I had a chance to notice that the anesthetic the doctor had given him, earlier in the day, was still functioning very effectively in my behalf.

A few moments later, I was able to recover my breath among some friendly beavers, who always received me with the greatest kindness.

At any rate, the story of my leap into the tiger's cage became known throughout the entire zoo in less than an hour, and this underground legend of my supposed bravery had the happy effect of keeping the local mouse population off my back from that time on.

Still, I did have a few other unpleasant adventures before the really great event of my whole life, finally, took place. For instance, there were some men employed in that park whose business it was to feed the animals, to clean the cages, and to try to prevent visitors from throwing dangerous objects through the bars.

After a time, I came to know two of these men pretty closely. One of them was called Peter, and when Peter first noticed me, I could see that, although my appearance seemed to cause him some surprise, he never made the slightest attempt to do me any harm.

The other caretaker was called Stooky, and his feelings about me were certainly quite different. This man never missed an opportunity to persecute me, and once, while I was quietly sunning myself on the lowest limb of a locust tree, he even managed to injure the tip of my tail with a rock he angrily hurled in my direction.

Well, as I've told you, things were going along in this way throughout the warm weeks of summer, and sometimes I used to wonder whether Bakaar was still pursuing

his Japanese studies with Doctor Yasakuchi or whether he had perhaps flown off, long ago, and returned to the Orient and had had a friendly reunion with that clever parrot in Pakotali. I often thought about Nancy and Martin, too, and hoped that perhaps someday I might see them again, if ever they should pay a visit to our zoo.

I realized, of course, that the summer couldn't last forever, and with the cold weather in mind, I had located a safe little retreat for myself right on top of a balcony in a quiet place that was a boiler room and tool shed combined. In one corner of this structure, there was also a small, glass-walled office, where a man called Mr. Cleland sometimes used to come and read his books and write things into ledgers, the way Doctor Howard used to do, in the old days, at the laboratory.

This Mr. Cleland was the head man at the zoo, and he was always on the most friendly terms with all the animals. He respected *them,* and they respected *him;* and once, when he accidentally happened to catch sight of me (in the kangaroo cage, where I had just delivered some dates), he gave a whistle of surprise, and later on I even heard him ask Peter about me. Luckily, it was this very kind man that Mr. Cleland happened to question.

"Oh, yes," said Peter. "I've seen him around for quite a few weeks now. It's hard to imagine where he could have come from. I myself think that some kid probably brought him along in a shoe box or something and that the little fellow just managed to escape somehow."

"That's more than likely," said Mr. Cleland. "Yes, indeed, that seems to me the most logical explanation for it."

Well, as I had been telling you, I had found myself a

70

warm and snug sleeping hole on a beam atop that balcony, right above Mr. Cleland's office; and the best part of these lodgings consisted in the fact that, since there was no food of any sort kept in this building, it was never visited by any mice.

There was one curious thing I discovered. Right near the staircase that led to this balcony, I noticed a small box with a little card in front of it, which was marked with an X, just the way some of the cards used to be at the laboratory. Actually, when I first saw it, I was almost tempted to push a button that was located right below this X; but I finally decided against it. My last experiences with button-pushing had not been so pleasant that I had any special reason for trying to repeat them.

AND now, if you are still listening, I am finally going to tell you about the tremendous event that happened to me just a little while ago.

It had been an unusually cool afternoon at the park; there hadn't been too many visitors that day, and when I had finished my supper, I decided to turn right in, without making any further visits even to those of my friends whose cages were quite close to my own quarters. I generally fall asleep rather quickly, and this evening, too, I was off to dreamland in no time at all.

And then, I don't know how soon after closing my eyes, I woke up and found myself shaken by a terrible coughing spell. I coughed so hard that my eyes were filled with tears, and when I at last staggered off my sleeping perch,

I realized that the whole place was completely filled with smoke. Suddenly, to my unspeakable horror, I saw a fierce red flame shooting out of a tool closet right below me, and in a few terrifying seconds, everything in the place seemed to be on fire. I trembled so hard that I fell off my high beam and landed on the banister that went all around that balcony. Not knowing what to do, I scurried toward the staircase; and just in order to avoid seeing those dreadful flames, I tried to crowd myself into a crack, right alongside that card-covered box I've already told you about.

And then an extremely strange thing happened to me: I suddenly decided that the best place for me to hide was behind that very card with an X marked on it, and so, without even a second thought, I gave a great big push to the button that was fixed below it.

The moment I had done this, an absolutely ear-shattering bell started to ring. It rang so loudly that its wild vibrations nearly shook me out of my skin. Meanwhile, the flames kept getting closer and closer, and since the card had failed to fall down, I made a desperate attempt to wedge myself into the very box that served as its frame and container. I suppose it must have been at this merciful point that I finally fainted.

When I came back to life again, the whole place was jammed with people. Most of them were shouting and splashing great streams of water over everything, and, what is more, everybody was wearing strange hats and shiny coats. But most important of all, that lunatic bell had at last given up its terrible racket.

And then, just as I was about to sneak out of my hiding

place, I saw Mr. Cleland standing right in front of me; and, what is more, he was looking me straight in the eye. Of course, I instantly tried to rush back into that box again; but it was no use. He reached out his hands and grabbed hold of me before I'd even had a chance to turn myself around.

As he lifted me up, I noticed that Peter, the good-natured zoo attendant, was standing right beside him, and I heard him say to Mr. Cleland, "Now, what in the world was *he* doing up here?"

"I'll tell you exactly what he was doing up here," said Mr. Cleland, who was holding me much less firmly. "He was setting off the fire alarm, that's what he was doing. And it's a pretty lucky thing for all of us that he managed to do it. I hate to think how much damage and suffering it might have caused if that alarm *hadn't* gone off."

"You really think it was *him* that did it?" said Peter.

"Who else?" said Mr. Cleland. "Believe me, I'd give quite a lot to know just exactly how it all happened. It certainly is a mystery, and chances are that you and I are going to be the only ones who will ever be wondering about it."

Well, Mr. Cleland was certainly quite wrong about that, because the fire marshal spread the whole story to the papers; and in the next few hours, I hardly had a moment's rest, what with all the photographers and news reporters, from different publications, flocking all over that zoo.

They kept snapping my picture and blinding me with their flashbulbs until I really thought I was going to get sick from the whole thing.

Of course, all this attention I received simply infuriated

the man called Stooky, who was all for having me drowned in a bucket of soapy water. "This varmint had nothing whatever to do with turning on that alarm," he told one of the reporters. "That bell is supposed to go off the minute the temperature gets over a certain point. I don't understand why everybody is making such a fuss about this measly, thieving sewer tramp. He should have been done away with long ago."

I can tell you right now that poor Stooky had some pretty tough days coming his way. You see, the newspapers all printed enormous pictures of me, and after Mr. Cleland and Peter had given interviews about all that had happened, the management announced that it would set me up in a little cage of my own, right near one of the outside windows of Mr. Cleland's private office.

WELL, believe it or not, I had become a hero.
That cage of mine turned out to be nearly an exact
duplicate of the one I had lived in at the National Research Laboratories; and every single day, hundreds of
people would come by and tap on the window, just to let
me know they were feeling friendly toward me.

But the most exciting thing that happened to me took
place the following Saturday morning, when Doctor
Howard and his two children turned up in Mr. Cleland's
office. It was Nancy who had recognized my picture in
one of the papers, because she had remembered the little
black spot on my left ear. Of course, no one had believed
her; but the moment Doctor Howard had taken a close
look at me, he was immediately convinced that Nancy was
quite right.

What a reunion! The children laughed so much and carried on so that, at last, Doctor Howard had to call a halt to their visit, for fear that so much excitement might be bad for all of us.

After they were gone, I had a short nap; and when, later on, I woke up and took a little refreshment, my mind kept constantly turning back to my friend Bakaar, who really deserved the credit for starting me off on my extraordinary journey into the world.

And then, Sunday evening, just as I was about to get settled down for the night, I heard a sharp rapping on the window in front of my cage; and when I looked up, there was Bakaar himself—long-beaked, shiny-feathered, and just as boldly black-eyed as when I had last seen him at the laboratory.

You can't imagine how I felt when I saw him standing out there on that window ledge. For a couple of moments, I actually didn't believe my eyes and thought I was dreaming the whole thing; but when Bakaar flew up to the half-open transom above the office door and dropped down beside my cage, I knew with joyful certainty that this marvelous visit was only too true.

"A very good evening to you, my brave and bonny buckaroo," he said. "The whole town is ringing with the sound of your adventures, and so I, too, could no longer resist paying my proper respects to so distinguished a public figure."

"Oh, my dear, dear Bakaar," I said, "you know best that I owe my whole life to you."

"Nonsense!" he said. "Let's rather talk about the Orient, for a change. You see, I am fully determined to go back to the Far East. I think I am really much better suited to life among the palm trees and the bamboo groves. During the monsoon season, when the heavy rains come down and inundate the earth, I'm quite prepared to let some amiable pasha or princeling provide me with a modest retreat for a little fruitful meditation. However, I don't want you to think that I intend leaving here without giving you due and sufficient notice. After all, you are the only close friend I shall leave behind me in this entire hemisphere."

That's how Bakaar talked to me until ever so late into the morning; and after he finally left, I was so happily exhausted that I instantly fell into a deep sleep, from which I didn't wake up until sometime on Monday afternoon. When I opened my eyes, I had good reason to suppose that I must have slumbered through a rather warm day, because I noted that Peter had left wide open the office window located right in front of my cage.

As I was quietly sitting on the edge of my blanket and staring aimlessly out into the park, I suddenly saw a mouse scampering across the asphalt road, and, surprisingly enough, it seemed to be heading straight in my direction.

Since I'd had no sort of dealings with any member of the mouse tribe for ever so long, I was naturally rather curious about the possible aims and intentions of my approaching visitor. I kept staring expectantly at my windowsill, and, sure enough, a moment later, a breathless mouse made its appearance just a few steps from me.

And do you know who this mouse turned out to be? No one else than that dear Tsi-Tsi who had given me such good advice and such kindly directions on the scary night when I had made my escape from the laboratory. I instantly recognized her, of course.

"Tsi-Tsi," I shouted, "how very sweet of you to come and see me. I'm sure your mother will be ever so furious if she finds this out."

"Oh, Mother knows all about it," said Tsi-Tsi. "In fact, she's waiting for me, at this very moment, directly across the road, right near the giraffe house."

"You mean to say your mother actually brought you here?"

"Well, not exactly," said Tsi-Tsi. "But, you see, when all of the mouse gossip around town was busy with nothing but you, and your name became known to everyone on the whole West Side, Mother could no longer pretend that you were just an obscure outsider. As a matter of fact, I even heard her mention to several of her friends that she had had occasion to meet you shortly before you started out on your special mission. Of course, she still refused to let me come and see you until she heard my grandfather announce that you certainly sounded like a first-rate campaigner and that, despite your color, for which no right-minded person could possibly blame you, the entire mouse population of the country had good reason to be proud of you. So when I again brought up the subject, she finally gave in, and here I am."

"And no one could be happier to see you than I, dear Tsi-Tsi," I said. "I've ever so often been thinking about you and wondering whether I would ever have the good fortune to meet you again."

"Ah, well," she said, "I'm sure you know a great many more important people now, and you probably think it was rather forward of me to call on you in this brazen fashion."

"Not at all," I said. "It's just like your sweet, impulsive nature to do exactly as your feelings dictate. I'm terribly proud and grateful that you took the trouble to make this long and dangerous trip just for my sake."

"Oh, I've been here three times before," said Tsi-Tsi. "We always came during the night, and since the windows of this place were always shut, we had to go away again. This building you live in scems very solidly constructed, and we were quite unable to find any sort of entrance at all."

"Yes," I said. "The mice in this zoo have never bothered to make passways into it, because there's never anything to eat in here, except, of course, inside my own box. By the way, Tsi-Tsi, may I offer you a little refreshment before you have to leave here? I still have some excellent Cheddar left from last night, and it will give me great pleasure to have you sample some of it. Please?"

Although it was plain to see that she would certainly have enjoyed having a small bite in my company, it took me quite a little while to persuade her to act on it. At last I did manage to convince her to climb to the top of my cage, which, as usual, consisted only of a loose piece of screening. I had no trouble at all in raising this makeshift covering, and a moment later, she had slipped in beside me.

Pretty soon, we were both nibbling away at the cheese and chattering along at such a great rate that we completely forgot about the rapidly passing time.

Indeed, I was so delighted by the conversation of my charming visitor that when Peter suddenly appeared out of nowhere, I actually became conscious of his presence only because of the loud noise he made as he banged down the outside window for the night. I hardly realized what the consequences of this action were likely to be.

Tsi-Tsi, on the other hand, instantly grasped the fatal significance of this event, and hurling herself headlong into the farthest corner of the box, she began to sob in the most heartbreaking manner. "I'm trapped!" she wailed. "I can't ever get out of here again! My mamma will have hysterics all over the West Side! Whatever is going to happen to me when these terrible zoo-people find me in here?"

Believe me, I was deeply shaken by her despair. What could I possibly do for her? How could I help her? What hope had I to offer for a happy solution to this horrible dilemma?

I flung myself down beside her and tried to whisper affectionate reassurances into her ear; but it was all in vain. She refused to listen. She sobbed, she wailed, she tore her hair and called herself every dreadful name she could think of. Over and over again, she continued to blame herself for the recklessness of her nature, which had propelled her into the midst of this awful catastrophe.

After a while, she became so exhausted by these exertions that she stretched herself out on my blanket, where she continued to whimper, spasmodically, for a long, long time.

I suppose that my helplessness, my terror, and the sight and sound of her grief had so completely worn me down that, for a short spell, I must surely have dozed off. That's the only way I can account for the fact that Mr. Cleland's face suddenly appeared right above me without my ever having heard him, either entering the office or approaching my box.

Not knowing what to do, I just made a pretense of not

noticing him at all, which was rather difficult, when you
consider that he was lighting up even the farthest corner
of my cage by means of an extremely powerful electric
lamp.

At last, after he had shut off this most unpleasant light,
he turned toward a shadowy figure standing beside him
and said, "You're absolutely right, Peter. The rascal has
certainly somehow managed to find himself a mate. I

really don't believe there's ever been such a mouse any-where in the world before. He runs away from a research lab; he moves into the zoo; he sets off a fire alarm; and now he's picked himself a local mouse and is going to raise himself a family, I suppose. Heaven only knows what other wonders he may still have in store for us. There's just one thing I want you to do for me, Peter. I don't want you to breathe a single word about this to anybody."

"I won't even tell my missis," Peter assured him solemnly.

"We have to keep this quiet," said Mr. Cleland, "because if those nosy newspaper people ever find out what happened, they'll all be right on top of us, worse than ever before."

"Well, you couldn't really blame them, either," said Peter, "when you think what a story they could make out of it."

"That's true enough," said Mr. Cleland. "So mum's the word, and let's say no more about it."

"Right you are," said Peter. "I'll just hang a cloth on the front side of his box and put a card in the window saying 'Closed for Repairs.' "

And that is exactly what was done; and for quite a while, everything was kept absolutely secret—until this morning, when, somewhere around ten o'clock, a fire inspector walked through this place; and shortly after he left, all the newspaper reporters and photographers in town started to hammer on our doors.

"I'm afraid we'll have to let them in," said Mr. Cleland. "This story is simply too big to be kept from people any longer. After all, how often does it happen that a mouse gives birth to sextuplets and that two of the litter turn out to be pure white, two of them all gray, and two of them are as speckled as a couple of uncooked poppy-seed rolls?"

Now, then, it may very well be that, at one time or another, you've already heard some part of this story; but all the true facts, *exactly* as they happened to me, have never before been told in this way until only just now.

THE END

about the author and artist

Alexander King (1899–1965) was born in Vienna. He came to the United States just before World War I with his father, a research chemist, and his mother.

Alexander King was the author of four best-selling memoirs. He had an illustrious career as author, illustrator, raconteur and television personality. In fact, his appearances on the Jack Paar Show captivated the audience and turned Mr. King into a nationwide celebrity.

Mr. King's wife, Margie, collects folklore and sings songs in many languages. She has made numerous television appearances with her husband, and she reads his and other children's stories on radio.

Richard Erdoes, also a Viennese, was born into a family of actors and opera singers in 1912. He studied at art academies in Vienna, Berlin, and Paris, and has received awards from the Art Directors Club, the American Institute of Graphic Arts, the Society of Illustrators, etc. A regular contributor to *Life, American Heritage* and other magazines, he is also active in the film, TV animation and advertising fields.

Now a citizen of the United States, Mr. Erdoes lives in New York with his wife, a fellow artist, and their three children.